Dewberry

and
the Lost Chest of Paragon

J. H. Sweet

Illustrated by Holly Sierra

SOURCEBOOKS
Jabberwocky
AN IMPRINT OF SOURCEBOOKS

Published by Sourcebooks Jabberwocky, an imprint of Sourcebooks, Inc.
P.O. Box 4410, Naperville, Illinois 60567-4410
(630) 961-3900
Fax: (630) 961-2168
www.sourcebooks.com

Library of Congress Cataloging-in-Publication Data

Sweet, J. H.
  Dewberry and the Lost Chest of Paragon / J.H. Sweet.
      p. cm. -- (The fairy chronicles ; bk. 11)
  Summary: When Dewberry and her fairy friends go in search of the Lost
Chest of Paragon, which is rumored to contain a great gift of knowledge for all
of mankind, the results of their discovery are far from what they expected.
  ISBN-13: 978-1-4022-1329-8 (alk. paper)
  ISBN-10: 1-4022-1329-8 (alk. paper)
  [1. Fairies--Fiction. 2. Magic--Fiction. 3. Conduct of life--Fiction.] I. Title.
  PZ7.S9547De 2008
  [Fic]--dc22
                                        2008002328

                    Printed and bound in China.
                    IM 10 9 8 7 6 5 4 3 2 1

To those who learn from their mistakes,
and to second chances

MEET THE

Dewberry

NAME:
Lauren Kelley

FAIRY NAME AND SPIRIT:
Dewberry

WAND:
Single Strand of Braided
Unicorn Tail Hair

GIFT:
Great knowledge and wisdom

MENTOR:
Grandmother,
Madam Goldenrod

FAIRY TEAM

Primrose

NAME:
Taylor Buchanan

FAIRY NAME AND SPIRIT:
Primrose

WAND:
Small, Black Raven Feather

GIFT:
Ability to solve mysteries

MENTOR:
Mrs. Renquist,
Madam Swallowtail

Snapdragon

NAME:
Bettina Gregory

FAIRY NAME AND SPIRIT:
Snapdragon

WAND:
Spiral-Shaped Black
Boar Bristle

GIFT:
Fierceness and speed

MENTOR:
Mrs. Renquist,
Madam Swallowtail

Inside you is the power to do anything

The Fairy Chronicles

Come visit us at fairychronicles.com

$\mathscr{C}$ontents

Chapter One

Dewberry and Her Research

The back yard of Lauren Kelley's house was perfect for adventures. With lots of trees, bushes, ground cover, and other dense foliage, there were plenty of places to hide, play, camp, and pretend. Like a lot of young girls, one of Lauren's favorite things to do was pretend. Today, she was wearing a striped beach towel for a cape and a cut-off bottom of a round fabric softener bottle for a crown.

The cape was pinned to the shoulders of her jacket, and the crown was perched slantways across her forehead over her short, curly black hair. Crouching between the crepe myrtle and the sage bushes, Lauren was awaiting a very special visitor. She backed up a bit to sit majestically on her throne—a flat chunk of limestone rock.

Lauren often sat on the limestone rock to read, write, and rule over her many queendoms. However, this morning she was not in the mood to sit idle and wait. She jumped up from her limestone throne and ran to the fence separating *her* yard from her grandmother's yard next door.

The special visitor was approaching, flying low over the distant treetops. Lauren waited patiently for her expected friend who was none other than Pegasus, the famous winged horse of mythology.

As the Muse of Scholarship, Lauren herself was endeared to Pegasus, and he frequently flew in to take her for long rides. Lauren climbed up onto the two-foot high garden retaining wall to mount the

beautiful white horse. She tripped a little on the rather long beach-towel cape, but managed to clamber onto his back nonetheless.

Off they went, soaring over houses and treetops (which were really dwarf holly bushes, backyard toys, and garden tools) on their way to the River of Wisdom.

Lauren was now the Queen of Knowledge, Sorceress of Wisdom, and Muse of Information. As overseer of the River of Wisdom, the Queen-Sorceress-Muse often made visits to the banks of the magical river, which had been created long ago by Pegasus' giant hooves gashing into the side of a mountain and releasing a flood of knowledge with the gush of fresh spring water.

Out of breath after running for nearly ten minutes, Lauren bid farewell to Pegasus, who rose slowly and gracefully over the neighborhood, departing for his home in the distant hills. Lauren then made her way up to the porch to have a drink from a glass of juice on the outdoor table. She waved at her grandmother who was visible through her kitchen window next door.

Lauren's grandmother often looked after her when her parents were out or busy. Today, her parents were visiting her aunt across town and running errands, so Lauren had the back yard all to herself. As long as she stayed visible to her grandmother's windows, she didn't have to check in very often.

The pretend play of Queen-Sorceress-Muse and riding on Pegasus was one of Lauren's favorite activities for a very special reason. In addition to being just like a lot of other girls, she was also a fairy and had been blessed with a dewberry fairy spirit.

In the standard fairy form of six inches high, Dewberry wore a soft green dress of creeping vines with tiny black dewberries nestled amongst the crinkled leaves. She also had small, misty green wings and wore soft slippers to match. On her belt, Dewberry carried a little pouch of pixie dust, the fairy handbook, and her wand, which was a single strand of braided unicorn tail hair. It glistened brilliant white and often made soft neighing, snorting, and whooshing sounds just like a unicorn.

Each young fairy was assigned a fairy mentor as a supervisor and teacher. The purpose of fairies was to protect nature and fix problems, so it was a tremendous responsibility to be a fairy. No fairy was ever allowed to use magic improperly. Fairy magic could not be used for trivial things. And young fairies were not supposed to use magic at all without permission from their mentors.

Dewberry's mentor was none other than her next-door grandmother, Beverly Kelley, who had been given a goldenrod fairy spirit. She was called Madam Goldenrod by most of the young fairies in the Southwest region, but Dewberry usually just called her Grandma. Sometimes, Dewberry and Madam Goldenrod attended special gatherings of fairies called Fairy Circles.

Lauren's parents did not know their daughter was a fairy, and fairy activities were kept secret from non-magical people. In fact, regular people could not even recognize fairies when they saw them because fairies in fairy form were only visible as their fairy spirits.

Madam Goldenrod was a very regal fairy, and rather stern. She wore a gleaming dress made of tiny golden flower petals that came almost to her ankles. Madam Goldenrod also had tall, autumn gold wings, and her wand was a tiny humming-bird feather. It was the smallest wand of

Madam goldenrod

any of the fairies and was a shimmering, greenish-blue color with a bit of purple tinge. Madam Goldenrod had short, silvery-white hair and wore oval gold-rimmed spectacles.

Each fairy was given a gift that was sort of like a strength or specialty. Madam Goldenrod's fairy gift was the ability to sense danger and deception. She had a heightened sense of caution and precaution, and could also make others tell the truth, if necessary. For this reason, she was slightly feared, and often avoided, by younger fairies. But Dewberry knew her Grandma would never use the gift of truth-telling lightly, so she didn't fear her at all.

Dewberry's special fairy gift involved great knowledge and wisdom, and she was dubbed the Fairy of Knowledge by other fairies. She could process information very quickly and knew legend as well as fact.

Dewberry was very much like a walking, talking set of encyclopedias.

Even at a young age, she was able to do research and learn things on her own. This helped tremendously in school. Due to her wealth of knowledge, she was at the top of her class. It was very likely that Dewberry would someday be valedictorian of her high school and would also probably graduate with honors from college. And she was already thinking about becoming a doctor when she grew up.

Unfortunately, there was a small glitch with Dewberry's fairy gift. The development of her wisdom had not quite started. True, she was full of knowledge. But she did not yet have the ability to make good decisions of exactly how to use the information properly. Madam Goldenrod recognized this in her grand-daughter, but Dewberry herself chose to ignore it. To be blissfully unaware of one's own faults made life much easier.

As a hobby, all during free time and playtime, Dewberry studied, researched, memorized, and puzzled over things. Then she studied some more, storing up massive amounts of knowledge. She was so hungry for information that she did little else.

However, she rarely used her fairy handbook because, quite frankly, it disappointed her. The handbook only gave her small bits of information. She could often find much more detailed explanations from other sources.

In truth, the handbook was doing exactly what it was supposed to do—limiting information for young fairies to just what was needed. The handbook took its job very seriously, and was forever trying to keep Dewberry out of trouble. However, Dewberry didn't think her conservative handbook was being helpful at all, so she usually ignored it and sought information elsewhere.

The previous summer, Dewberry had gone on a fairy adventure to the River of Wisdom, where she was introduced to the Library of the Ages floating above the river. With several fairy friends, she had helped to rescue the librarian, a nymph named Sage, from the Spirit of Ignorance. Unfortunately, Dewberry did not know the location of the River of Wisdom because they had traveled to and from the river in a magic golden elevator.

It was actually a good thing that Dewberry couldn't make her way to the river. If she had been able to find it, she likely would have been so drawn to the immense cache of knowledge that she would have probably never returned home. And, of course, a nine-year-old girl could not be permitted to endlessly camp out on the banks of a magical river far from home.

However, Dewberry had figured out how to access materials from the Library of the Ages. During their visit, the fairies had learned that bits and pieces of knowledge are delivered to mankind by way of swifts, who carry the library materials to and from the river. So it was a simple thing for Dewberry to befriend a large family of swifts in her neighborhood and request the frequent delivery of select information needed for her study.

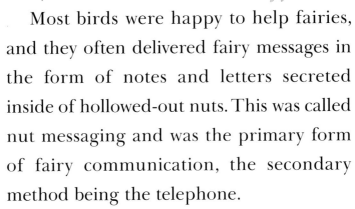

Most birds were happy to help fairies, and they often delivered fairy messages in the form of notes and letters secreted inside of hollowed-out nuts. This was called nut messaging and was the primary form of fairy communication, the secondary method being the telephone.

Dewberry had already achieved a claim to fame among her fellow fairies, and had been highly praised by Madam Toad, the leader of fairies for the Southwest region. For decades, it had been a great mystery as to why fairies were afraid of jigsaw puzzles. Fairies could not stand to do jigsaw puzzles, and if faced with one, they were often bewitched by the puzzle, becoming trapped in it. Inside the puzzle, fairies would follow the curving lines, tracing them over and over again, often never making their way out unless helped out by a witch, elf, or some other magical creature. Occasionally, another fairy could help, but only if quick enough and brave enough to bear the effects of the puzzle for as long as it took to pull out the trapped fairy.

The answer to this mystery lay in a goblin curse. Dewberry had discovered the legend in a musty old book called *Sixty-Three-and-a-Half Goblin Tales*. The jigsaw puzzle tale was number forty-two, and told of the anger of a lady goblin toward a dandelion fairy who had tricked the goblin into releasing two captured boy fairies, also known as brownies.

Dandelion had been carrying a jigsaw puzzle with her on her way to a friend's home to play, when she stumbled across the goblin and brownies. Dandelion helped the brownies get free, making the goblin very angry. The goblin had noticed that the fairy was carrying a puzzle and had performed the clever *Fairy-Puzzle-Trapping-Curse*, just as the brownies and fairy escaped from her.

The fairy and brownies were unaware of the curse. When Dandelion tried to piece together her jigsaw puzzle that afternoon while visiting a fairy friend, both fairies became trapped in the puzzle. Fortunately, a garden gnome noticed the trouble and brought a witch to help them.

Since then, the warning had been passed

down from generation to generation for fairies to avoid jigsaw puzzles. However, the story of the brownies, goblin, and curse had been forgotten or left out of the telling for many years. Thus, the mystery had begun, unraveled only by Dewberry.

This was a cold Saturday morning in mid-January, and it was a three-day weekend due to the Martin Luther King Jr. Holiday.

After reciting the "I Have a Dream" speech earlier for her grandmother, Dewberry gave herself permission to play Queen-Sorceress-Muse for a while. Later in the morning, two of her fairy friends, Primrose and Snapdragon, were coming for a visit.

For almost a year, Dewberry had been researching the Legend of Paragon. This had been a particularly difficult story to piece together. In fact, there were still huge chunks of it missing. However, Dewberry had gathered enough information to guess at the blanks and make up things to fill in the holes so that the story made sense to her. Since she now had what she thought was enough information, Dewberry was planning to ask Primrose and Snapdragon for their help in seeking the Lost Chest of Paragon, rumored to contain a great gift of knowledge for all of mankind.

Paragon was an ancient ruler and a great scholar. The information Dewberry had gathered involved a legend recorded by Exemplar, one of three marshals working for Paragon. Exemplar's job involved researching, advising, and recording information.

Paragon's kingdom had been at war with a neighboring land. A legendary gift of knowledge had just been unearthed by Paragon's other two marshals—Apotheosis and Criterion. Paragon feared that the knowledge might fall into the hands of his enemy, to be used against him, or for ill purposes, so he ordered his marshals to lock the knowledge away in a chest and hide it for safety.

This was done, and the means to find the chest was kept secret to make it difficult for anyone to locate it. Paragon intended to seek the chest later to put the knowledge to good use for the betterment of mankind. However, the neighboring army killed Paragon and his three marshals. Thus, no one knew where the chest was hidden or how to find it.

Dewberry had read bits and pieces, here and there, about Paragon, his marshals, and the chest. She desired very much to locate this gift for mankind and achieve even greater fame among the fairies. Also, if she could contribute something to the world with the discovery of hidden and valuable knowledge, she would finally feel that her fairy gift was truly being put to good use.

She had discovered the latest part of the legend two days before, when a swift delivered a parchment scroll to her. Finally, Dewberry had enough information to act, so she immediately sent nut messages to Primrose and Snapdragon, asking them to come over on Saturday for an adventure.

Chapter Two

The Map of
Apotheosis

While waiting for her friends to arrive, Dewberry searched the back yard for Mr. Ruble, the garden gnome, who usually came on Saturdays to tend to the plants, shrubs, and trees. Gnomes were responsible for helping to make things grow and adding colors to nature.

Regular people couldn't see gnomes because gnomes used disguise magic to prevent detection so they could go about their business undisturbed. To non-magical people, Mr. Ruble would simply look like a watermelon, a rolled-up water hose, a soccer

ball, a pumpkin, a sandbox toy, or some other object that didn't look out of place in a particular yard or garden.

Mr. Ruble had wisely decided to bypass the Kelley yard today when he noticed Dewberry playing Queen-Sorceress-Muse. He often avoided her, returning late at night, or at different times, when Dewberry was otherwise occupied. Mr. Ruble was a wise and knowledgeable garden gnome, extremely skilled in his craft. In fact, he was considered an expert in coloring various squashes and fruits. So it was very tiring for him to listen to long lectures from the know-it-all fairy, advising him on his job techniques. It was much nicer to work in peace. Mr. Ruble had nicknamed the Kelley property his *"midnight yard"* since that was the time when he most often visited it these days.

Primrose arrived first. Her real name was Taylor Buchanan, and she had wavy blond hair. As a fairy, Primrose wore a dress made of translucent pink flower petals, and she had tiny gold wings. Her wand was a black raven feather, and her special fairy gift was the ability to solve mysteries. She could easily pick up on small details to figure things out quickly. Primrose was always able to work out who the criminals were in mystery books before the detectives barely even had a clue.

Dewberry took off her cape and crown when Snapdragon arrived. Then she went inside to get cookies and juice for her friends.

Snapdragon's real name was Bettina Gregory. In fairy form, she wore a dress made of yellow and orange, furled snapdragon petals, and she had bright orange wings that were tall and wispy. She had light brown hair and carried a boar bristle wand that was curled like a corkscrew. Her special fairy gift involved fierceness, with the ability to protect and defend when necessary. She was also gifted with speed, and could fly nearly as fast as a dragon. Madam Swallowtail was mentor for both Primrose and Snapdragon.

Primrose and Snapdragon both waved to Madam Goldenrod, still visible at her window keeping an eye on things. Madam Goldenrod waved back. She was writing letters while watching Dewberry. As long as she could see her granddaughter fairly frequently through the window, she didn't need to check on her in person. Dewberry knew that she could go in and out of her own house through the back door to get things as needed, but if she wanted to spend a long time indoors, and out of sight, she would have to do it at Grandma's house, or convince Grandma to come over, because those were the rules.

As soon as her guests were settled at the back porch table with their cookies and juice, Dewberry launched into the story of the Legend of Paragon and his lost chest. She told them everything she had discovered about this great mystery gift for mankind, and how Paragon and his marshals had used ancient magic to unearth these secrets.

The girls speculated for a while, as to what possible knowledge the chest contained.

"Maybe it's a cure for cancer," suggested Primrose.

"Or diabetes, or epilepsy, or cystic fibrosis," added Snapdragon hopefully.

Primrose had another idea. "Maybe it's a blueprint for World Peace," she said.

The girls were very excited about the many possibilities.

Next, Dewberry told her friends that the first step to locating the chest would be to seek the Map of Apotheosis. "Apotheosis was Paragon's chief carto- grapher," she said. "He made maps of all of the territories under Paragon's rule. The last scroll I reviewed about the legend said that all grebe birds know the location of the map. Evidently, grebe birds are somewhat magical. They keep this knowledge and pass it down through the generations."

Dewberry was breathless with excite- ment as she went on. "Now grebe birds do not live in this area, so the only place nearby we can find one is at the zoo. I already convinced Grandma to drop us off at the zoo when she finishes her letters. And she is okay with my plan that we secretly change to fairy form behind bushes in the park next to the zoo and fly ourselves home. That way, we can be free to take the next step after the map, if we can figure out what that next step is."

Dewberry was beaming at her friends with anticipation. She thought her plan was excellent. However, Snapdragon and Primrose were looking at each other skeptically.

"Have you told Madam Goldenrod what you are doing?" asked Snapdragon. "Researching the legend and seeking the chest? It might be good to consult a mentor, or at least your handbook, before embarking on this quest."

Primrose nodded. She certainly would have liked Madam Swallowtail's opinion about all of this before going forward.

But Dewberry shook her head. "Other than flying, we won't be using any fairy magic. Fairies are allowed to fly around without a mentor's permission. This is strictly a treasure hunt," she argued. "Except for getting some of the legend information from the River of Wisdom, which regular people also have access to even if they don't know it's a magical river and library, there is nothing fairyish going on here. The swifts would have delivered the same information to anyone else, if it was needed or requested."

What Dewberry said made sense. So both Primrose and Snapdragon agreed to go along with her plan, even though they were a little uneasy about it.

Madam Goldenrod stepped out onto her own back porch and called to the girls. "I'll be ready in five minutes. Make sure you put the glasses and plates in the sink, then meet me in the driveway." The girls hurried to do this and were ready to go when Madam Goldenrod emerged from her front door, locking it behind her.

As they neared the downtown zoo, something in the facial expressions of both Primrose and Snapdragon set off Madam Goldenrod's precaution sensor. The girls looked reluctant, nervous, and worried all at once. Dewberry just looked thrilled, so Madam Goldenrod wondered what her granddaughter might be up to. As she gave the girls money for the zoo entrance fees and snacks, she also gave them a warning. "Just a reminder—flying is the only fairy activity you are approved for on your own. Only in an emergency would you be allowed to use any other magic without a mentor present."

The three girls all nodded their understanding, but Snapdragon and Primrose still looked somewhat troubled.

The zoo wasn't very crowded since it was mid-winter. Having visited many times, Dewberry knew exactly where the bird exhibit was located, and they had no trouble finding the grebe bird in his own native habitat enclosure. He was at the far corner of his pen, pacing back and forth behind some shrubs and scratching the ground for seeds and bugs.

Adorned with beautiful gray-and-white plumage, the grebe bird was around the size of a large turkey and had dark gray feathers forming a crest on the top of his head.

"I wonder how we should go about this," said Dewberry, doubtfully. "Now that we are here, it seems silly to talk to a bird in a zoo about a map."

"I thought your last clue said all grebe birds know about the map," said Snapdragon.

Dewberry nodded. "Yes, but since birds can't talk, unless they are bewitched, how would this one be able to tell us about the map, even if he knows where it is?"

"I suggest the direct approach," said Primrose, a little impatiently. "Just ask him," she added, nudging Dewberry's shoulder.

"Um..." began Dewberry, looking around to make sure there were no other

zoo patrons nearby. "Uh…Mr. Grebe Bird, can you tell us how to find the Map of Apotheosis? We are seeking the Lost Chest of Paragon."

To the fairies' surprise, and delight, the grebe bird stopped pacing and looked directly at them. Next, he gave them a slow wink as a tiny glass tube, only about two inches long, magically appeared at Dewberry's feet. She picked it up quickly, and the grebe bird went back to his scratching and pacing.

Inside the tube was a very small map, extremely detailed. Dewberry put the map back in the tube for safekeeping. Then she slipped it into her pocket, telling her friends, "We will need to be in fairy form to read this because it's so small."

The girls left the zoo and made their way into the nearby park, taking cover behind a dense growth of oleander bushes.

Dewberry took the glass tube out of her pocket and removed the map. Then, with three little *pops*, the girls changed into fairy form. The map was now the correct size for them to see clearly with their tiny fairy eyes.

Before they began studying the map, Snapdragon brought up a good point. "If we had to change into fairy form to read this tiny map, then this is a fairy activity, not just a simple treasure hunt. Maybe we should consult a mentor before pursuing the chest further."

Primrose nodded in agreement.

However, Dewberry had an answer, as always. "Nonsense," she said, "I could have gotten a magnifying glass like a regular person. This just saves time." (Dewberry had obviously decided to ignore the fact that the map had appeared magically out of nowhere: something that wouldn't have been easy to explain away as normal.)

One of Dewberry's hobbies was studying maps, along with everything else she studied. There were no words on the map; rather, it contained very distinctive geographical markings of rivers, mountains, woods, rocks, and trees. The map also showed the location of the Obelisk of Criterion, which would hold the next clue to finding the chest.

It didn't take Dewberry long to recognize the landscape of the map. "This is just on the outskirts of the Forgotten Forest," she said.

The Forgotten Forest was part of the Howell Nature Preserve and was restricted to the public. "See where these two streams come together, just like Coyote Wash and Henderson Creek," said Dewberry. "And they travel around the base of a hill on the edge of this valley, just like the landscape of the basin area of the preserve."

Dewberry was very excited to have worked out the map so quickly. All her hours of pouring over area maps had not been wasted. However, she was a little discouraged. "We're almost thirty miles from the preserve," she told her friends. "That's too far for us to fly. I guess we'll just have to wait until we can plan an outing, and we may have to involve our mentors to be able to travel that far."

Primrose and Snapdragon were somewhat disappointed too. They had also been excited when Dewberry worked out the map so quickly.

Just as the fairies were thinking of starting for home, two brownies arrived behind the bushes, riding on a rabbit. Since brownies couldn't fly, they often rode on birds and animals to travel.

These brownies were twins named James and John, also known as Donnybrook and Ruckus because brownie

twins always had nicknames. Snapdragon and Primrose had met them before, at a special fairy gathering the previous summer near the Cave of Courage. Dewberry had never met the twins. James and John introduced themselves to her after saying hello to Snapdragon and Primrose.

Brownies and fairies were usually wary of one another because brownies often delighted in playing tricks on fairies. However, there had been a good relationship for the last two years between the fairies and brownies of the Southwest region, and they had worked together on several successful missions.

Brownies got their spirits from earthy things like mushrooms and mosses. James and John were both granite rock brownies and had reddish-brown hair and lots of freckles. They were dressed in the brownies' traditional tan colors and wore strings of polished granite chips around their necks.

"What are you guys up to?" asked John curiously.

It was somewhat unusual to find fairies in public parks. They usually stayed in normal girl form unless they were on a fairy adventure. And public parks were not common places for fairy adventures. Rather, it would be more likely for fairies to be found out in the wilderness somewhere.

Dewberry didn't tell the brownies her ultimate goal of locating the Lost Chest of Paragon. Instead, she explained that she was seeking an obelisk marked on a map. "Unfortunately," she added, "we can't get there. It's too far for us to fly."

"We can help you with that easily!" exclaimed James. He then gave a sharp whistle and looked toward the sky.

The fairies and brownies watched the sky and waited. After a few minutes, two hawks arrived; at which point, the rabbit took off in a hurry through the bushes.

The girls were very excited at the prospect of riding on hawks.

"We can go with you as far as the preserve," said John, "but then we'll have to leave, or risk being late for a brownie meeting."

Primrose and Dewberry rode behind John on the first hawk, and Snapdragon rode behind James on the second. It was quite cool and windy high in the air, but the fairies held on tightly and were warm enough nestled in the silky hawk feathers. Dewberry carefully carried the glass map tube, tucked tightly under one arm.

Chapter Three

Criterion's Obelisk

As they flew, Dewberry explained that Criterion was Paragon's head field marshal and was in charge of all military operations. "He marked all of Paragon's territories with giant stone obelisks like the one shown on the map."

When they arrived at the place where the two creeks came together on the edge of the preserve, Dewberry consulted the map again. The obelisk drawn on the map was shaped like a tall, thin tower with a pointed pyramid at the top. The location of the monument was a point on the northeast side of a clearing near the entrance of the basin.

Unfortunately, it seemed that the map had led them to a dead end. There was no obelisk in the clearing. Where it should have been, a tall Spanish oak tree stood instead.

John was looking over Dewberry's shoulder at the map. "Hang on," he said. "Let me try something." He ran to the oak tree and walked around the trunk three times. As the others approached the tree, John gazed up at it, smiling. "There it is," he said.

The rest of the group thought John might have gone a little crazy. All they could see was the oak tree. "Look at the map closely," he instructed. Around the base of the obelisk on the map, encircling it, were three lines with arrows pointing in a counter-clockwise direction.

"Oh," said Dewberry. She led, while Snapdragon, Primrose, and James followed. When each of them had circled the tree base three times counter-clockwise, the tree no longer looked like a tree but was instead an immense stone obelisk. It had been magically disguised somehow.

"Well, we have to go," said John.

As the brownies climbed onto one of the hawks to get ready to leave, James told them, "The second hawk will take you home when you are ready." Then, blushing a little, he added, "Please tell Cinnabar I said hello." It was well known that James liked Cinnabar, a moth fairy, very much.

The girls nodded and thanked the boys. Then the hawk took off, soaring high, and the brownies waved to the fairies below. The other hawk waited patiently in the distance for them.

Dewberry next turned her attention to the obelisk. It was a pale gray color and was as tall as the oak tree had been, about twenty feet high. Near the top of the pointed stone monument was a carving. It was not easy to see from the ground, so the fairies flew up to look at the markings.

As they ascended, Dewberry told her friends, "We could have gotten a ladder, but this saves time." By now, Snapdragon and Primrose were so keyed up about the quest that they were less concerned about rules than before.

The carving on the obelisk was clearly the shape of a rock formation. Again, Dewberry recognized it. "It's not too far from here," she said excitedly. "We won't need to ride on the hawk, but we will need him to take us home afterwards."

Dewberry flew to the hawk, explained where they were going, and told him that they probably wouldn't need to stay there very long before they would be ready to go home. He nodded his understanding and took off in the direction the fairies were also heading. Brownies and birds had a very good relationship with one another. The brownies had requested help transporting the fairies, and the hawk wasn't about to leave them stranded. He was very reliable.

The hawk was waiting for them fifteen minutes later when the fairies arrived at the very distinctive, twin towering rocks extending from the base of a cliff on the side of a small mountain.

The shape of the obelisk was carved very small into one of the two giant rocks, near the bottom. Directly below the carving sat a large, solid black, glittering rock. None of the fairies had ever seen a rock like this before.

"I think we'll have to move it to find the chest," said Snapdragon. "I bet it's underneath."

"But we will need to be in girl form to do that since we can't use magic," Primrose reminded them. Snapdragon and Dewberry nodded.

With three *pops*, the girls were standing over the black rock. The stone was heavy,

but it was also flat, so the three of them managed to lift it without serious strain. They propped it up on its side against the larger rock.

Underneath the black stone was indeed the Lost Chest of Paragon.

Chapter Four

The Chest of
Paragon

Dewberry carefully took the chest from the indentation under the rock and placed it at her feet, peering at it intently. It was actually quite small, about the size of a standard recipe card box. Then the girls changed back into fairy form and stood in front of the chest to examine it. It was very ornate and was made of a bright, silver-colored metal that was not at all tarnished. Since the chest was still shiny and beautiful, the fairies decided it must be made of some unknown metal, or perhaps protected from weathering by some kind of magic.

The lid of the chest was inset with four different-colored stones in four distinct shapes: a red tornado, a blue lightning bolt, a yellow fireball, and a green S-shape.

Just as Dewberry was reaching to open the lid, Primrose stopped her. "Look at the black stone," she said. "We didn't notice. It has carvings underneath."

"Oh," said Dewberry, examining the carvings. "They're petroglyphs: pictures and symbols carved into rocks. How interesting. This is how they used to record history, decorate, and send messages because paper and parchment weren't available."

The symbols carved into the stone resembled four human figures, each holding a different-shaped object in his hands. The objects looked like a tornado, a bolt of lightning, a fireball (or sun), and something S-shaped and wispy like a snake made of smoke. The four figures were holding out the objects, as if offering them to an invisible someone.

The black rock also contained several small drawings below the petroglyphs. Pointing, Dewberry told her friends, "And these are pictographs. They are drawn on, instead of being carved into the rock."

The pictographs looked as though they were done with a kind of bright red dye; the color stood out noticeably in contrast to the black rock. The drawings appeared to represent many human figures lying down, either asleep or dead.

"What do you think it means?" asked Snapdragon.

Dewberry thought for a while before she answered. "It looks to me like the four carved figures are about to heal the lying down figures, like they have a cure for their illnesses."

Primrose was looking thoughtfully at the markings, and shaking her head. "Or the four might have hurt the others with the objects they are holding in their hands."

For some reason, Primrose suddenly felt extremely uneasy about this whole situation. "I think we should leave the chest alone for now, Dewberry," she said, "and consult an older fairy. Something isn't right here."

Snapdragon stepped forward immediately and said, "I agree." She trusted Primrose's judgment and was also feeling very unsettled about the chest and the rock markings.

However, Dewberry was determined. "We've come this far; we can't quit now. This is a great gift of knowledge for mankind."

Primrose and Snapdragon still looked skeptical, and they backed up a few steps.

Dewberry stared at her friends' uneasy faces and sighed. "If I don't understand what's inside when I open the chest, we will leave it here and consult a mentor. Okay?"

Neither Primrose nor Snapdragon nodded. They just glanced at each other worriedly.

But Dewberry was not to be stopped. She mumbled to herself as she lifted the lid of the chest. "But there's not much danger of my not understanding what's inside, since I *am* the Fairy of Knowledge."

As the lid of the chest opened, Dewberry's face glowed brightly with the reflection of the colors of the contents. Her cheeks, forehead, and nose all sparkled brilliantly with glints of red, blue, yellow, and green light. Then she stood back from the chest, smiling at her friends.

Four glittering clouds rose from the chest simultaneously in the forms of a red tornado, a blue lightning bolt, a yellow fireball, and a green snakelike wisp. Rising slowly into the air, each of the four clouds went in a different direction. Then, each one split into a hundred smaller identical clouds and began moving away in the sky, very fast.

Before the girls lost sight of the four groups of clouds, they noticed that the shapes divided themselves again into more hundreds. The moving multitudes of colored clouds were very faint for a while, then the fairies lost sight of them completely.

Dewberry turned to her friends, looking puzzled. "I don't feel any smarter," she said, "and I don't think I have gained any more knowledge. Maybe I was supposed to grab one each of the clouds before they moved away."

Primrose and Snapdragon just looked scared when Dewberry added happily, "But as fast as they seemed to be multiplying, I'm sure the whole world will be enjoying the lost knowledge by tonight, or tomorrow, at the latest."

$\mathcal{P}$undit $\mathcal{P}$eriphery
and the Real Legend

Primrose and Snapdragon were still silent a few moments later when Dewberry pondered, "I guess we should ask the hawk to take us home now."

The girls glanced around for the hawk and were troubled to discover him nowhere in sight. They hadn't noticed, but at the very instant Dewberry opened the chest, the hawk was watching, horrified. He took off in fear, and haste, just as the first four clouds had risen into the air.

The fairies didn't have long to worry. Barely a moment after they discovered that the hawk had vanished, a lynx, with a small man riding on his back, bounded up to them. The man wasn't like an elf or a dwarf. He was simply a very small man, just the right size, in fact, to be riding on the back of a lynx. The man was also bald and a bit wrinkled.

"Oh dear!" he exclaimed in a rather high-pitched voice for a man. "Oh no! This is terrible," he added, sliding off the lynx.

The lynx was a golden brown color with dark gray speckles and spots, and he had a short tail. As soon as the man dismounted, the cat leapt to the top of a small boulder and lay down, watching over them. His pointed, furry-tufted ears twitched as his rider began speaking again.

"I am Pundit Periphery," the tiny man squeaked. "It has been my task for many years to keep the knowledge of how to locate the Lost Chest of Paragon scattered and hidden, so that no one would be able

to find it. Somehow, you have pieced it all together and located the chest." Mr. Periphery shook his head in agony, shuddering, as he wailed, "Not only have you found it, but you have opened it!"

Mr. Periphery abruptly sat down on the ground cross-legged as he moaned, "What is to be done?" Wringing his hands, he looked sharply at the girls, exclaiming shrilly, "Fairies! I would have never believed this of fairies! How old are you anyway? And where are your mentors? This is terrible!"

Primrose was the first to be able to speak. "Please, Mr. Periphery. I am ten. My friends are nine. Our mentors don't know that we are here. But we don't understand what has happened. Please tell us what is wrong."

Mr. Periphery looked slightly more calm, but none less stern, after Primrose addressed him.

"Sit down with me," he said, indicating the ground in front of him. As the three fairies took their seats, he continued. "Most people call me Mr. P. You may too, if you like."

Sighing deeply, he went on. "It has been my job for many long ages to keep the details of the Legend of Paragon out of the hands of inquisitive people who are susceptible to temptation. You might have some knowledge of the history of Paragon, but you probably do not know the truth.

"King Paragon was a conqueror, an evil tyrant who was never satisfied with simply ruling over his own kingdom and torturing his own people. He sought out neighboring kingdoms to conquer and new people to torment. Paragon believed that he was superior to other human beings and that he was born to dominate them."

Wide-eyed, the fairies listened carefully as Mr. P continued. "Paragon had three marshals working under him—Criterion, Exemplar, and Apotheosis. They were just as terrible and horrible as their leader. Together, they exerted cruelty and oppression over all of their subjects. In the interest of their military strategies and conquering techniques, they consulted dark witches and wizards, and did much research into ancient magic. They bargained with Malatrocious, the Specter of Evil, and obtained dark secrets from several demons working for him.

"Paragon obtained a weapon in the form of multiplying curses from four of the specter's servants: demons who specialize in hunger, conflict, drought, and disease. Paragon hoped to overcome many enemies with these specific evils. He stored the collected curses in this chest."

Mr. P's shaking hand lightly touched the top of the chest as he went on.

"Unfortunately, for him, Paragon was unable to use the curses quickly enough to conquer an invading army. A neighboring country had recognized Paragon as a threat and had organized several armies into one to try to stop him. Before Paragon could use his secret weapon, the invasion had begun.

"Fearing that the opposing army might find a way to use his own weapon against him, Paragon hid the chest, intending to seek it out later when reorganizing and planning his own advances. However, the invading army took no prisoners. They killed Paragon and his marshals, along with everyone else. But the map and obelisk survived; and Exemplar, before he died, managed to record clues of how to locate the map, the first link to finding the chest.

"Now, let me tell you what the real problem is." Mr. P sighed as he continued. "As I said, the chest contained powerful curses constructed by demons in control of hunger, conflict, drought, and disease. The Specter of Evil and his demons bargained with Paragon to help him conquer his enemies with these vicious tools. Of course, Paragon didn't know that these dark spells would have eventually overcome his own peoples too. Darkness and evil are powerful vacuums, and they are never satisfied with just a bargain."

Mr. P's voice was both stern and sorrowful as he again addressed the young fairies. "Since you released the ancient curses, all of mankind will now suffer. Where food was plentiful, there will now be hunger. In places of peace, conflict will now prevail. Drought will take over lush areas of the planet, making them barren and inhospitable. And illness will spread rampant over the earth. Human beings and animals will suffer terrible pain and misery from this. Opening the chest means the end of everything that is good in this world."

The fairies all stared at Mr. P in horror.

Primrose's chin quivered, and Snapdragon was struggling to say something, but she had a huge lump in her throat, and all she could manage was a gasp.

Dewberry was shocked, but was not quite as troubled as her friends. She looked from one to the other, then she put her hands together, rubbing them lightly as she addressed Mr. P. "Okay, so what do we need to do to fix this?" she asked.

Mr. P just stared at her. And so did Primrose and Snapdragon. Even the lynx glared at Dewberry from his position on the rock above.

Shaking his head unbelievingly, Mr. P said, "You think this can be fixed? Did you not understand what I just told you?"

Primrose and Snapdragon were looking at Dewberry sadly, as though it were the end of the world. But Dewberry just looked confused, and she was very persistent. "There has to be a way to fix this," she said. "It was caused by ancient magic, right? There are always ways to fix problems caused by magic with more magic. Just tell us what to do, or tell me where to look for the answer."

Shaking his head again, Mr. P answered. "The magic was contained. It was right where it was supposed to be. None of those curses can ever be canceled or destroyed or reversed. They are too strong—too full of evil. Magic did not cause this problem," he said, his voice straining. "You did. You worked very hard to piece together information that was purposefully hidden. And you ignored the warning on the rock. When you opened the chest, you released something that is unstoppable. There is nothing you can do."

Dewberry stood up quickly, her face white, and she wandered a few steps away from the others. Panic and shock were now overtaking her. She couldn't breathe. There was no reason to doubt what Mr. P had just told her, except that because she had caused this problem, she must somehow find a way to fix it. *She Must!* Her face was now flushed and red as she gasped for air and said, "I...but...there has to be some way."

She had no time to ponder further because an owl had just arrived carrying Brownie Christopher, leader of the brownies, along with Madam Toad, Madam Swallowtail, and Madam Goldenrod.

The instant the chest had been opened, the hawk, sensing terrible danger, had contacted Brownie Christopher, who had then sought out Madam Toad.

The young fairies were very relieved to see their mentors and their fairy

leader. And at this moment, they weren't even fearful of their own consequences regarding their actions. They were just hopeful that the older fairies would be able to sort everything out.

Chapter Six

The Mentors' Council

M r. P engaged briefly in conversation with Madam Toad before departing on the lynx. Madam Goldenrod told the girls to fly onto the owl's back. He was kindly going to take them all home. Brownie Christopher left the gathering riding a small red fox that had appeared suddenly, out of nowhere, at the base of the rock cliff.

Dewberry, Snapdragon, and Primrose said nothing on the trip home. They were each dropped off at their own individual houses and instructed to speak to no one about what had happened.

With the girls safely at home, the mentors proceeded to Madam Toad's house on Belvin Street. Madam Toad was really Mrs. Jenkins, and she lived in a large, three-story historic home. In addition to Madam Swallowtail and Madam Goldenrod, Madam Finch and Madam Monarch were also able to attend the meeting to try to help sort this mess out.

Already, certain parts of the world were being affected by the evil curses. Illnesses were springing up, causing pain and suffering. Drought was drying up lakes and riverbeds, and settling over places that normally had lush vegetation growing this time of year. Fighting among ordinarily peaceful peoples had begun. And stored food was beginning to rot.

After reviewing the various spells and magical abilities of the fairies, Madam Toad and the others came to the conclusion that no one in the realm of fairies could fix the problem. No fairy wand was strong enough, and no amount of pixie dust could fight the spreading evil.

Upon learning about the trouble, Madam Toad had immediately consulted a kindly witch named Drucilla, and had asked her to request help from among other witches, if possible, to solve this problem. Unfortunately, Drucilla arrived at the mentors' meeting and informed Madam Toad that she had talked to fellow witches, both light and dark, and that none of them could think of a solution. The witches could try to help cure individual illnesses, but they could not battle this problem on the larger scale. Neither light nor dark magic of the witches held the answer to fighting the demons' curses.

Similarly, Madam Toad had already talked to a dwarf, a leprechaun, and a gnome before departing to retrieve the three younger fairies.

The dwarf, leprechaun, and gnome representatives all arrived together and expressed the same problem the witch had reported. No magic in their communities was powerful enough to provide a solution. However, the gnomes did know some food preserving spells, since they did a lot of canning and drying. And they would also gladly share some of their stored food to help combat starvation, if needed. But, of course, this would only be a temporary solution. Gnome storerooms would empty quickly once the curse of hunger became more widespread.

Madam Toad's final hope rested with the elves, the oldest and wisest of all magical creatures.

An elf named Trace arrived in answer to Madam Toad's summons. He had helped the fairies on a mission before. Trace appeared out of thin air in Madam Toad's

parlor just as the dwarf, gnome, and leprechaun were leaving.

After the situation was explained to him, Trace left briefly to consult with other elves. He returned ten minutes later and told the fairies, "The Elder Elves agree with me that the only answer is to consult Mother Nature directly. There really is no other choice. I know her current location, and I will take you to meet with her. But we must do this quickly. If there is any way to stop the spread of the curses, Mother Nature must get involved right away."

Chapter Seven

Mother Nature's
Decision

Mother Nature was the guardian of magical creatures and the supervisor of all activities of nature. Madam Toad agreed with Trace, but she was not especially looking forward to meeting with Mother Nature. The only previous meetings Madam Toad had had with the fairy guardian, Mother Nature had initiated herself. It was extremely troublesome to seek her out.

Madam Toad didn't particularly want to admit that one of her fairies had caused this problem, even though there was no denying it. She had hoped to solve the matter herself without involving Mother Nature. Mother Nature could take any form of nature and was often in dangerous forms such as tidal wave, mudslide, and volcanic eruption. No one could ever be sure of meeting her in a safe form like sea foam, fog, or morning dew.

Madam Goldenrod and Madam Swallowtail agreed to make the trip with Madam Toad. Since their own fairy charges had caused this terrible problem, they weren't about to let Madam Toad face Mother Nature alone.

Trace readied the fairies for the elf *Travel-Sleep-Spell*. "You will need to dress warmly," he said. "It is cold where we are traveling to."

The fairies all bundled themselves in the warm cloaks that they often used for their winter outdoor fairy activities. Madam Toad's cloak was a silky greenish-brown color. The cloak Madam Swallowtail wore was a soft, velvety black. And Madam Goldenrod had a deep, mustard-yellow satin cloak. The fairies fastened the garments tightly around them. When they arrived at their destination, it would take forty-five minutes for them to come out of the *Travel-Sleep-Spell*.

Just our luck, thought Madam Toad, *Mother Nature is probably in blizzard form. But I guess we deserve this for not keeping a closer eye on Dewberry.*

Elf travel was instantaneous. Trace carefully watched over the sleeping fairies for the forty-five minutes needed for them to come out of the spell. It had only been late afternoon when they left Texas, but it was very dark when they arrived in Alaska because sunlight was scarce in that part of the world during the wintertime.

Trace stood a little ways off from the fairies, waiting to take them home after their discussion with Mother Nature. He didn't want to interrupt, and he didn't feel the need to give input. Trace knew that Madam Toad was capable of looking after herself in this type of situation.

However, it was a few moments before Madam Toad or the other fairies could speak because they were absolutely entranced by the sight of Mother Nature. She was in the form of the Northern Lights, also called the aurora borealis. Soft ribbons of colored light fluttered across the sky, glittering and undulating in red and blue rippling waves, almost like ghosts dancing over the hazy clouds and under the twinkling stars. Mesmerized by this sight, the fairies were not even cold. The trance was broken when Trace cleared his throat, which was a good thing or the fairies might have stared forever, forgetting the reason for their visit.

Once she came back to her senses, Madam Toad spoke right away. "Mother Nature, the fairies need your help to fix

a terrible mistake. Dewberry opened the
Lost Chest of Paragon. Demonic curses
were released and are now spreading
over the earth. Hunger, conflict, drought,
and illness will soon overcome us all."

Madam Toad also briefly explained the details of all of the events that occurred, including the meeting at her home. Then she paused and waited apprehensively with the others for a response.

When Mother Nature spoke, her voice was deep and earthy rich, reverberating through the trees. And the sound seemed to come from both the sky and the ground at once. "There is no magic that can fix the problem you describe. The curses should have stayed contained in the chest. They are unstoppable curses. No being, earthly or otherwise, could cancel that type of magic. Even the demons who created the curses could not reverse them. Too much evil is involved."

Mother Nature paused for a few moments before continuing. "Go back to your home," she finally said. "I will think over the matter and join you there in one hour."

Trace accompanied the ladies home right away. Forty-five minutes later, when the fairies were again conscious, he left, requesting that Madam Toad send him a nut message later telling of Mother Nature's decision.

Mother Nature arrived fifteen minutes later, as promised, in the form of cold winter rain. The fairies stayed on Madam Toad's back porch, protected from the pounding wetness.

Mother Nature addressed them in her clear, rich voice, which was now a bit watery and splashy. "I will leave the matter of how to deal with Dewberry entirely to you.

"A magical creature caused this situation, even if she did it without direct use of magic, so I *can* offer a solution to the problem. The answer is a *Repeat Day*. I have only ever used this time-altering magic on one other occasion, to rectify another problem, which I cannot share with you. At midnight, the day that has just occurred will repeat itself. Of course, in different parts of the world, the day begins at different times, so it will affect people all over the world for the twenty-four hour time period that coincides with your repeat Saturday."

The fairies nodded their understanding as Mother Nature went on. "Beginning at midnight, your time, individuals all over the world will experience the events of the last twenty-four hours over again without realizing what is happening. Since they do not know that time is repeating, in theory, people should do exactly the same activities they did before, so there will be very little effect on the future.

"Only those who are aware of the problem will remember both days. This includes your fairies, Mr. Periphery, and the select elves, gnomes, witches, dwarves, leprechauns, and brownies that you consulted. You have about five hours, until midnight, to inform everyone involved of what is to happen. Tell them to repeat as many of their Saturday actions as possible, exactly as they occurred.

"Of course," Mother Nature added, "I hardly need to tell you the exceptions to the repeat actions. There can be no quest to seek the chest. The young fairies should stay carefully, and quietly, away from any activities that were involved in the finding of the chest."

Madam Toad, Madam Swallowtail, and Madam Goldenrod were all very relieved to have a solution placed before them. They hastily thanked Mother Nature, who disappeared into the night with a loud crack of thunder.

Next, the mentors set to work quickly, sending nut messages with rabbits and birds in the back yard to all of the parties in question, warning them of the *Repeat Day* and telling them to exactly copy their actions to the best of their abilities with the exception of any activities or discussions involving the chest.

Then, Madam Swallowtail went to seek out Primrose and Snapdragon, while Madam Goldenrod traveled home to speak to her granddaughter.

Chapter Eight

Dewberry's Fate

In the morning, it was Saturday again for Dewberry, which was confusing, but necessary.

Madam Goldenrod had arrived at her granddaughter's home the night before at just about bedtime, and around the time Dewberry's parents were getting extremely worried about their daughter's unusual behavior that evening.

When Dewberry, as Lauren, had arrived home from the trip to the zoo that afternoon, her parents were back from running their errands. Though it was common for Lauren to shut herself in her room, reading for hours, it was unusual for her not to be able to swallow more than about two mouthfuls of her favorite dinner—spaghetti with meatballs. And it was also strange for her not to be able to communicate more than just with nods and shakes of her head. Clearly, she was upset over something.

When Grandma arrived, she convinced Mr. and Mrs. Kelley to let their daughter sleep, and assured them that everything would be fine in the morning. It had just been a tiring day. She hoped this would be enough information for Dewberry's parents since they wouldn't remember the day anyway come midnight.

Then Madam Goldenrod went in to talk to Dewberry and tuck her in. To alleviate her granddaughter's worries, she briefly explained what was going to happen and told Dewberry that they would talk tomorrow, Saturday, while Dewberry's parents were out.

This was such a relief to the young fairy—that there was a solution to the problem she had caused. She was able to fall asleep, free from most of her anxiety.

Early Saturday morning, Dewberry had breakfast with her parents, the same one she had had on the original Saturday. Then her parents left to run their errands, and Dewberry went out onto the back porch to wait for her grandmother. She sat with her cape and crown, but did not put them on to play Queen-Sorceress-Muse. Since she had been alone when she played the previous day, she didn't think it mattered that she didn't repeat the exact play activities.

Grandma Kelley had gotten up early to make sure she rewrote all of the letters she wrote the previous day. She was glad to get

that activity out of the way so she would have time to talk with her granddaughter. Before Madam Goldenrod left Madam Toad's house the previous night, the fairy leader confirmed that the decision Madam Goldenrod had made about Dewberry's fate was acceptable. As soon as the letters were deposited in the mailbox, Grandma Kelley went next door.

Dewberry sat quietly, waiting for her grandmother to begin speaking. Madam Goldenrod sighed a little as she began. "Do you remember how disappointed you were not to be chosen as leader of the River of Wisdom mission?" she asked.

Dewberry nodded as her grandmother continued. "I remember what you told me when you got back: that the Spirit of Ignorance was such an idiot, any fairy could have easily tricked him into giving up the nymph. Since that time, you have been very anxious to prove yourself. And you have worked hard. I was so proud of you for discovering the answer to the jigsaw-puzzle mystery."

Madam Goldenrod leaned forward and gave her granddaughter a hug. Then she asked Dewberry another question. "Do you know the most common age young fairies discover that they are fairies?"

Dewberry shook her head as her grandmother answered the question. "It is usually somewhere between seven and ten years of age. However, I am going to tell you a secret. Some fairies will never learn that they are fairies. There is a purple tulip fairy that lives just three blocks from here. She is twenty years old. But she is silly, selfish, and very spoiled; and she is incapable of making good decisions most of the time. It takes a tremendous amount of maturity to accept the responsibility that comes with being a fairy. She may never be ready to handle it.

"It was my decision to tell *you*," Madam Goldenrod continued, "when you were eight. I thought that living next door, I could keep a close eye on you. Plus, I had never been chosen to be a fairy mentor before, and I was anxious to get started. In a way, I wanted to prove myself too, and be successful, in the same way that you have a thirst to prove yourself. I realize now that you were told too early."

Dewberry couldn't resist an interruption. "But Teasel and Pumpkinwing are younger than I am, and they were told at age six that they were fairies."

"Each girl matures at a different rate," Madam Goldenrod responded. "And as I explained, there is no set time when fairies are told about their fairy spirits.

"Even though you thought you were acting outside of the magical realm, your fairy gift of the ability to discover information and acquire knowledge so easily gave you the means to find out the details about the legend of the lost chest. Due to the skill of Mr. Periphery in hiding the secrets of the legend, it is very unlikely that another human being could have pieced the clues together to actually locate the chest. I know you didn't believe magic was involved," Madam Goldenrod added kindly. "You thought there was simply lost knowledge in the chest, so you are not entirely to blame.

"It is actually remarkable that you accomplished what you did, and under different circumstances you would be given high praise for your cleverness and hard work. You have talked about becoming a doctor someday. Imagine what your gift could allow you to do in that profession. Your research alone may be responsible for curing currently incurable illnesses. Or you may discover some miracle for safe and easy weight loss, or pain-free childbirth.

"However," Madam Goldenrod's tone became sterner, "your impulsive nature on this occasion can earn you no praise. You didn't stop to question your actions; you just plowed on. The inability to stop and question, especially when you didn't understand everything, indicates a serious lack of judgment. You never stopped to consider why the chest was so well hidden. If it was supposed to be such a great gift for mankind, why wasn't it made available to the world before now? When you saw the petroglyphs and pictographs, why didn't you stop and find out their exact meaning before opening the chest?"

Madam Goldenrod allowed this information sink in, and let Dewberry ponder for a few minutes, before she went on. "Do you see my point?" she finally asked.

Dewberry nodded reluctantly. She very much understood her grandmother, and she was beginning to fear what her consequences might be for acting with-out thinking first. "Are Primrose and Snapdragon in trouble too?" she asked.

Again Madam Goldenrod sighed. "Do you think they should be in trouble?"

"No," answered Dewberry immediately. "They just went along with me. They didn't cause this problem. And they warned me several times to stop and consult my hand-book or a mentor. I wish now that I had taken their advice."

Madam Goldenrod was nodding. "It is a good sign that you are able to learn from your mistakes. Primrose and Snapdragon will be given a warning; but otherwise, they are not in trouble. Fairies are almost always given a second chance when they make a mistake before their fairy spirits are taken away from them and their memories altered to forget all fairy knowledge."

Dewberry was holding her breath, hopeful that she would be included in the category of "fairies given a second chance." She continued to listen attentively as her grandmother went on. "Your fairy spirit is not going to be taken away from you, and there will be no memory alteration."

Dewberry barely had a chance to breathe a small sigh of relief as her grandmother added, "However, I am going to take your wand and handbook from you for one year. And you will not be able to participate in fairy activities for the rest of this year. You *will* be allowed to attend December's Christmas Fairy Circle since it is nearly a year away. Then I will give you back your wand and handbook next year on this date. For the time that you are without them, I want you to concentrate on doing well in school, like you always do, and think carefully about taking action only when you have full information. This will give you time to learn patience and develop wisdom to go with your knowledge."

Dewberry nodded. So far she agreed with everything her grandmother (and fairy mentor) had told her. "Are my wand and handbook really disappointed with me?" she asked.

Madam Goldenrod shook her head, smiling. "Of course not," she answered. "They love you. But I wonder if you can tell me all the purposes of your fairy handbook."

Dewberry thought for a few moments before answering. "It gives me information, answers questions, and advises me. But also, its purpose is to limit information until I am ready for it. When I am older, I will understand things better and be able to make wiser decisions, so I will be able to handle the more complex information.

"If I had consulted my handbook about the lost chest," Dewberry went on, "I probably would have discovered how dangerous it would be to open it. Even if the handbook didn't know the details about the legend, it would have known that I needed to be careful and would have warned me."

"Good answer," said Madam Goldenrod, nodding.

Shortly after Madam Goldenrod went back next door, Primrose and Snapdragon arrived to visit Dewberry, just as they had on the original Saturday. The girls had cookies and juice together, but they didn't go to the zoo. Since they had only visited the grebe bird, and the zoo had not been crowded, there wasn't much danger that they would have an impact on anyone else's future by not going to the zoo.

The girls played games together in the back yard and talked about boys at school. Primrose was a year ahead of Dewberry and Snapdragon, but they all attended the same elementary school.

Dewberry told her friends that she would not be attending Fairy Circle again until Christmas. Even though Primrose and Snapdragon were sad about this, they were happy that nothing worse was going to happen to Dewberry.

Grandma Kelley drove Primrose and Snapdragon home at about the same time the girls had been dropped off on the original Saturday.

Dewberry was quiet in the car on the way home from dropping off her friends. She was thinking about everything that had happened on the two Saturdays that were really one.

It was funny how much older she felt. She was thankful that her mistake had been fixed, and she *had* learned from it. Even though she would miss fairy activities during the upcoming year, she was looking forward to practicing being careful and wise about her actions.

On Saturday evening, Dewberry was able to enjoy her repeat spaghetti and meatball dinner.

But something else very strange happened as a result of this experience. Dewberry, who had never feared anything, was suddenly cautious of all boxes, chests, and trunks. She wasn't at all curious anymore about what was in her aunt's cedar chest or her father's travel trunk. In fact, Dewberry wasn't even sure she liked shoeboxes anymore. People stored things in them, and it was troublesome to think that they could contain almost anything, or at least anything small enough to fit into a shoebox.

It seemed that Dewberry had all of a sudden developed caution, which tempered her curiosity somewhat. Though it was odd not to wonder about things, or investigate as much as she used to, after awhile, Dewberry decided this change was okay, and that it must have something to do with growing up.

The End

Fairy Fun

From the Fairy Handbook

Why Fairies are Afraid of Jigsaw Puzzles: Fairies cannot stand to do jigsaw puzzles. If faced with one, they are often bewitched by the puzzle and become trapped in it. Fairies follow the curving lines, tracing them over and over again, sometimes never making their way out of the puzzle unless helped out by a witch, elf, or some other magical creature. Occasionally, another fairy can help, if quick enough and brave enough to bear the effects of the puzzle for

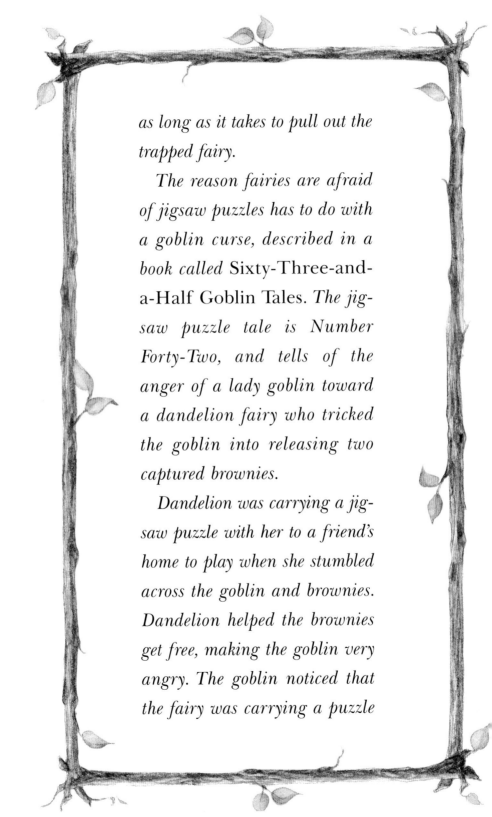

as long as it takes to pull out the trapped fairy.

The reason fairies are afraid of jigsaw puzzles has to do with a goblin curse, described in a book called Sixty-Three-and-a-Half Goblin Tales. *The jigsaw puzzle tale is Number Forty-Two, and tells of the anger of a lady goblin toward a dandelion fairy who tricked the goblin into releasing two captured brownies.*

Dandelion was carrying a jigsaw puzzle with her to a friend's home to play when she stumbled across the goblin and brownies. Dandelion helped the brownies get free, making the goblin very angry. The goblin noticed that the fairy was carrying a puzzle

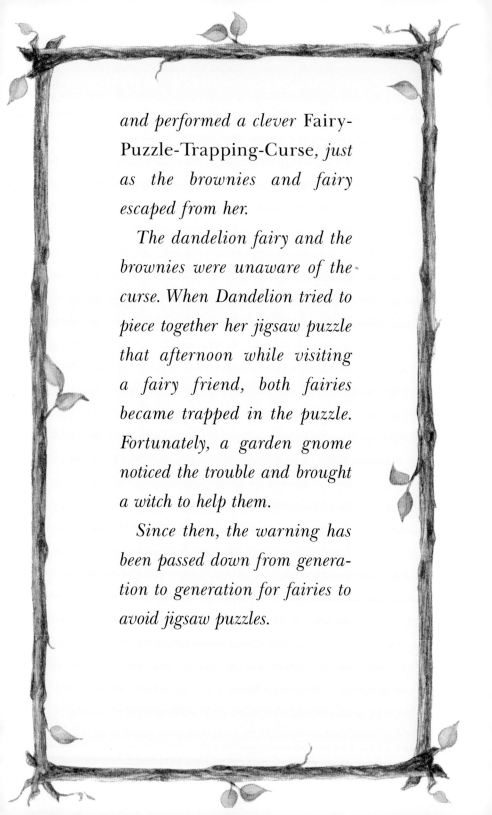

and performed a clever Fairy-Puzzle-Trapping-Curse, *just as the brownies and fairy escaped from her.*

The dandelion fairy and the brownies were unaware of the curse. When Dandelion tried to piece together her jigsaw puzzle that afternoon while visiting a fairy friend, both fairies became trapped in the puzzle. Fortunately, a garden gnome noticed the trouble and brought a witch to help them.

Since then, the warning has been passed down from generation to generation for fairies to avoid jigsaw puzzles.

From *Sixty-Three-and-a-Half Goblin Tales*

by Odious V. Nastia, lady goblin
and storyteller:
Tale Number Forty-Two
"Why Fairies Fear Jigsaw Puzzles"
Or
"That Dratted Dandelion and Those Blasted Brownies"

Those blasted brownies were in my clutches. I had them locked in a parakeet cage, which is the most fitting place for a couple of nasty, over-grown, mischievous boys. They were only there two hours though before that dratted dande-lion fairy came along. I was just stirring up a vat of Very Venerable Vittles, intending to add the brownies when the gravy was thick enough, when Dandelion popped by my hut unexpect-edly. She had been on her way to a friend's house to play. At first she acted like she had smelled my vittles stew and just could not resist stopping in to share recipes with me. She tricked me! Never listen to a fairy's cooking advice. I told her I was using my grandmother's recipe, and that it had always turned out very tasty. However, that dratted Dandelion managed to convince me that I needed to add tarragon to the recipe, because that was the way her grandmother used to make Very Venerable Vittles. So I had to climb up the stepladder to reach the tarragon. While my back was turned, Dandelion performed an *Unlocking Spell* on the parakeet cage. Then those blasted brownies threw handfuls of pepper at me, making me sneeze so much that I couldn't catch them while they jumped out the window and rode off on a rabbit. In my sneezing fit, I also upset my lovely vat of Very Venerable Vittles. But I got them good in the end. That dratted Dandelion was carrying a jigsaw puzzle—*yes, she was*—and when she flew off just after the brownies escaped, I took out my Spell Stick (sometimes I call it my Curse Club) and enacted the *Fairy-Puzzle-Trapping-Curse*. I had one of my spies follow her, a crooked rook he was, and he came back and told me that Dandelion and her friend both got trapped in the puzzle that very afternoon. Serves them right! But a gnome noticed what had happened and brought a witch to help them. So what! Eventually, the curse will spread to all jigsaw puzzles because that is the way I designed it. Well, I don't like to brag, but nothing can ever undo a curse like that, done by me. I plan to polish my medal every year in February over that one, I can tell you. Forever more, fairies will have to either avoid jigsaw puzzles or get trapped in them. Pretty sad for them, if you ask me, because jigsaw puzzles are actually a lot of fun. Ha!

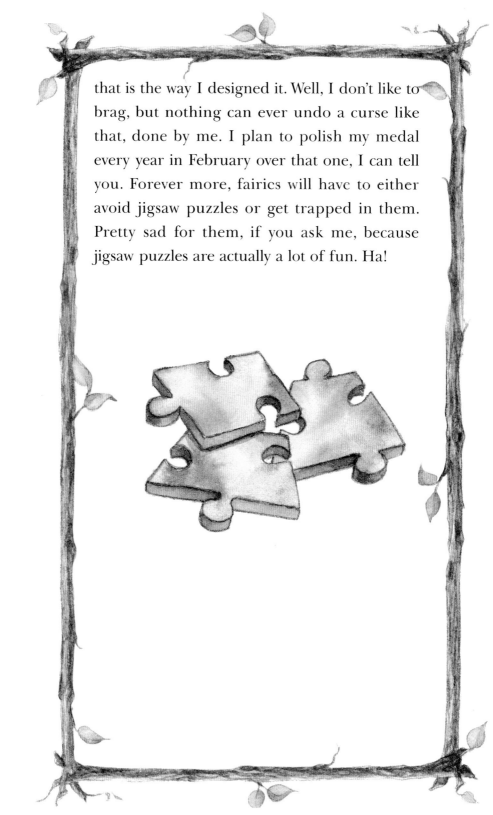

Pegasus

Though all winged horses are called Pegasus, the original Pegasus was believed to be the son of Poseidon, who was both god of the seas and god of horses, and a gorgon monster named Medusa. Athena, the goddess of wisdom, caught and tamed Pegasus. The winged horse then became the servant of several water nymph spirits known as the Muses, who inspired arts such as dance, poetry, and music. One legend of Pegasus depicts his assistance to the Muses as that of creating springs of artistic inspiration in each of the places his hooves touched the earth. Pegasus also carried lightning bolts for Zeus and helped Eros bring in the dawn. He once aided a hero named Bellerophon who was able to gain Pegasus' assistance by using a golden bridle given to him by Athena. Since Pegasus was not immortal, like the gods, Zeus decided to transform the winged horse into a constellation on the last day of his life, to forever be a part of the heavens.

Petroglyphs and Pictographs

Petroglyphs are rock images made by carving or engraving. Sometimes called rock art, the oldest petroglyphs date back to around twelve thousand years ago. Since a great variety of petroglyphs have been discovered, many theories exist to explain their purposes. Depending on where the rock images were found and the content of the pictures, some were believed to be an early form of writing for communication and storytelling purposes. Other petroglyphs have been connected with the study of astronomy. The rock art also appears to have been used for religious ceremonies and musical performances. Similarities in styles of petroglyphs on multiple continents have

116

led historians to a better understanding of the migration of our ancestors.

Pictographs, sometimes called pictograms, are images drawn or painted on rocks. This type of rock art is believed to have originated in China. Throughout history, the images and symbols of pictographs varied greatly in both content and complexity, causing as much speculation for their different uses as the explanations developed for petroglyphs. However, pictographs were most often created for specific useful purposes such as recording family histories and giving directions, as opposed to art for beauty's sake or decoration only. Totem poles are considered to be a wooden version of pictographs. Though not often drawn or painted on rocks, many street signs and advertisements of today also fall into the category of pictographs, proving that some very old traditions can still be very useful.

The adventures
don't end here!

Come visit us at
www.fairychronicles.com

for even more
fairy magic
and fun!

- 🐞 Become a Fairy Chronicles member
- 🐞 Upload your own fairy drawings
- 🐞 Read about all of the *Fairy Chronicles* adventures—and get sneak peeks of the next books
- 🐞 Meet each fairy and learn more about your favorite characters
- 🐞 Help protect Mother Nature with cool recycling activities and ideas
- 🐞 Check out the online Fairy Handbook as well as trivia, recipes, poems, and crafts
- 🐞 Download special bookmarks, computer graphics, and more free stuff
- 🐞 Send your friends *Fairy Chronicles* e-cards

And much more!

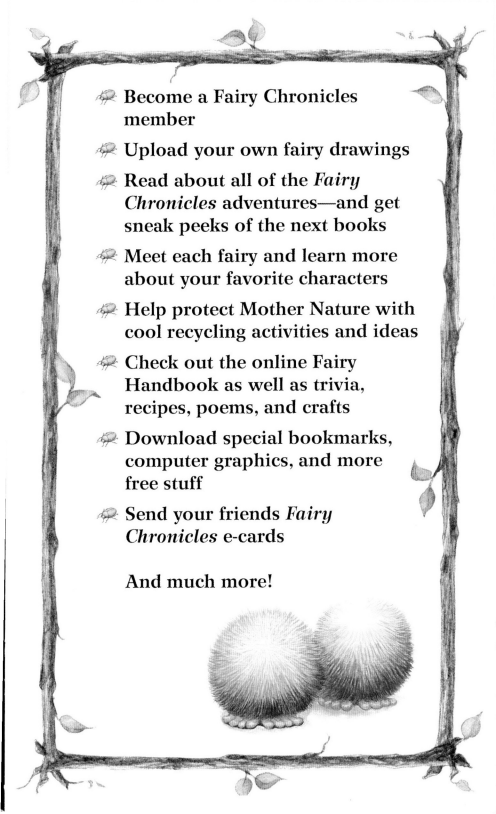

About the Author

J.H. Sweet has always looked for the magic in the everyday. She has an imaginary dog named Jellybean Ebenezer Beast. Her hobbies include hiking, photography, knitting, and basketry. She also enjoys watching a variety of movies and sports. Her favorite superhero is her husband, with Silver Surfer coming in a close second. She loves many of the same things the fairies love, including live oak trees, mockingbirds, weathered terra-cotta, butterflies, bees, and cypress knees. In the fairy game of "If I were a jellybean, what flavor would I be?" she would be green apple. J.H. Sweet lives with her husband in South Texas and has a degree in English from Texas State University.

About the Illustrator

Holly Sierra's illustrations are visually enchanting with particular attention to decorative, mystical, and multicultural themes. Holly received her fine arts education at SUNY Purchase in New York and lives in Myrtle Beach with her husband, Steve, and their three children, Gabrielle, Esme, and Christopher.